OKOMI
Climbs A Tree

Helen and
Clive Dorman

Illustrated by
Tony Hutchings

Dawn Publications
in association with The Jane Goodall Institute

It was early morning.
Okomi and his mommy,
Mama Du, were on one of
their walks. It had rained
during the night. All around
them, leaves sparkled with
drops of water.

Okomi spotted a branch
with some tasty new leaves
high up in a tree.

Okomi had seen his mommy
climb trees to pick leaves.
He was feeling adventurous
and wanted to try, too.

Okomi had climbed small trees
before, but this was a tall tree.
Bravely, Okomi began
to inch his way up.

The wet tree trunk gleamed.
It was very slippery.

Oh! Be careful Okomi,
you nearly fell!

The branch was finally close.
Okomi grabbed for it—but
missed, and started sliding
down backwards!

Okomi slid down and down,
faster and faster, clutching
the tree as tightly as he could.
Thud!

"Hoo, Hoo, Hoo!" he whimpered.

Okomi wasn't really hurt.
He had landed on soft leaves.

Mama Du looked over at Okomi,
but kept on eating.
She was used to his bumps.

Okomi sat very still, looking at
the wet tree trunk in front of
him. Then he looked up at the
branch with its nice, juicy
leaves. He got up and started
to climb the tree again.

First, he put one arm around
the tree trunk, then one leg.
Then the other arm,
and then the other leg.
Okomi used all his strength.

Up and up he went.
Nearer and nearer
came the leaves.

Okomi grabbed the branch!
Well done, Okomi!

Okomi ate the tasty green
leaves at last.
Proudly he sat on the branch
high above the ground.

Soon Okomi had finished
his meal and wanted
to get down.

Oh, no!
How could he get down?
He was stuck!
Okomi was frightened.
He held on tightly and
whimpered loudly.

Mama Du had been keeping an eye on Okomi, so she was not surprised when he started whimpering.

Mama Du climbed the tree.

She tried to lift Okomi off the branch but he was clinging on too tightly.

Poor Okomi was getting more and more frightened and tired. Mama Du kept gently persuading Okomi to let go.

Finally he sprang into her arms, safe at last. Mama Du had rescued him! He grunted softly as she cuddled him for a long time on the branch.

By now, the sun had dried
the tree trunk.
Okomi felt brave again and
climbed down all by himself.

Well done Okomi, you did it!

The Work Of Jane Goodall

For many years, Jane Goodall patiently watched chimpanzees in the African forest. She saw chimp babies play with their mothers and that chimpanzees have close family ties. She saw young chimps throw tantrums and have exciting learning adventures. She saw that the chimpanzee mother-infant relationship is virtually identical to its human counterpart.

Jane Goodall's research of more than 40 years showed how chimpanzees reason and solve problems, how they make tools and use them, and how they communicate. It revealed that they have a wide range of emotions. It showed that each of them has a unique, vivid personality. Indeed, their genetic makeup is closer to us than any other animal—with almost 99% identical DNA. Jane's revolutionary work bids us to look upon chimpanzees as non-human relatives.

Jane with an orphan chimpanzee

Photo by Michael Neugebauer

Yet the plight of these "relatives" is desperate. Their forests are being cut down. They are being hunted for food. Their numbers are dwindling drastically. And when chimpanzee mothers are killed, the orphaned babies—often taken to be sold illegally as pets—cannot be returned successfully to the wild.

When Jane realized that chimpanzees were becoming endangered, she began a worldwide effort on their behalf. She campaigns tirelessly, and established The Jane Goodall Institute. It has created sanctuaries for orphan chimpanzees. (You can help the orphans by "adopting a chimp.") It works to improve conditions in zoos and laboratories, and to halt deforestation and the bushmeat trade. The Institute also

Fanni and her baby, Fax.

sponsors Roots & Shoots, a worldwide program for young people working to make a difference for animals, the environment and their communities. For more information contact The Jane Goodall Institute, P.O. Box 14890, Silver Spring, MD 20910, or call (301) 565-0086, or go to www.janegoodall.org.

Part of the proceeds from the sale of this book supports the work of The Jane Goodall Institute's Tchimpounga Sanctuary in the Congo Republic. Dawn Publications is dedicated to inspiring in children a deeper understanding and appreciation for all life on Earth. To view our full list of titles, or to order, please visit our web site at www.dawnpub.com, or call 800-545-7475.

A Sharing Nature With Children Book

Published by arrangement with The Children's Project Ltd., P.O. Box 2, Richmond, TW10 7FL, U.K., and the Jane Goodall Institute Ltd., 15 Clarendon Park, Lymington, Hants SO41 8AX, U.K.

Library of Congress Cataloging-in-Publication Data

Dorman, Helen.
    Okomi : climbs a tree / Helen and Clive Dorman ; illustrated by
Tony Hutchings.
        p. cm. -- (A sharing nature with children book)
Summary: As his Mama Du looks on, Okomi, a young chimpanzee, tries to
climb a very tall, slippers tree to reach some tasty leaves.
    ISBN 1-58469-045-3 (pbk.)
    1. Chimpanzees -- Juvenile fiction. [1. Chimpanzees--Fiction. 2.
Animals -- Infancy -- Fiction.] I. Dorman, Clive. II. Hutchings, Tony, ill.
III. Title. IV Series.
    PZ10.3.D7185 Ok 2003
    [E] -- dc21
                            2002015159

Dawn Publications
P.O. Box 2010
Nevada City, CA 95959
530-478-0111
nature@dawnpub.com
www.dawnpub.com

Printed in Korea

10 9 8 7 6 5 4 3 2 1
First Edition
Design and computer production by Andrea Miles